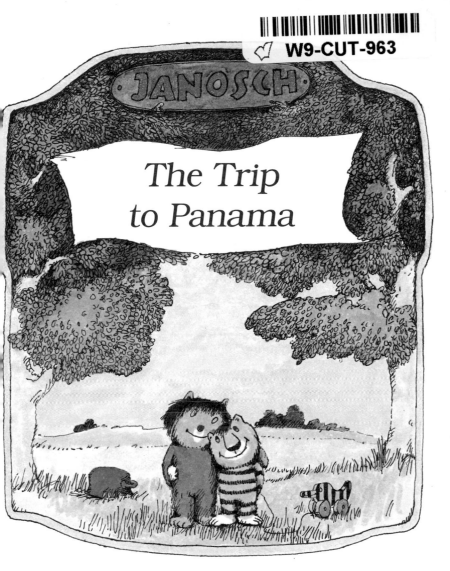

The Trip
to Panama

Translated by Anthea Bell

BELTZ
& Gelberg

Deutscher Jugendbuchpreis 1979

Gullivers Bücher (74)
© 1978, 1982, 1990 Beltz Verlag, Weinheim und Basel
Programm Beltz & Gelberg, Weinheim. Alle Rechte vorbehalten
Ausgabe in englischer Sprache
für die Bundesrepublik Deutschland, Österreich und die Schweiz
© der englischen Übersetzung bei Andersen Press Ltd., London
Reihenlayout und Einband von Wolfgang Rudelius. Einbandbild von Janosch
Gesamtherstellung Druckhaus Beltz, 6944 Hemsbach
Printed in Germany
5.90.1
ISBN 3 407 78074 5

Once upon a time, a little bear and a
little tiger lived down by the riverside.
Where you can see smoke rising into the
air, beside the big tree.
They had a boat too.

They lived in a nice little house with a chimney.

»How happy we are!« said Little Tiger. »We have all we could wish for, and we don't have to be afraid of anything. That's because we're so strong, aren't we, Bear?«

»Yes,« said Little Bear. »I'm as strong as a bear, and you're as strong as a tiger. That should do.«

Every day, Little Bear took his rod and
went fishing and Little Tiger went out in
the woods looking for mushrooms.

Little Bear cooked their dinner every day,
because he was a very good cook.

»Would you rather have the fish cooked with salt and pepper or lemon and onion, Mr Tiger?«

»All of them!« said Little Tiger. »And I want the biggest helping!«

After the fish they ate stewed mushrooms, and then they had bilberry jam and honey. They really did lead a very happy life in their nice little house down by the riverside. Until one day...

...a crate came floating down the river.

Little Bear fished it out of the water, sniffed it, and said, »Oooh...bananas!« The crate did smell of bananas. And what was that word written on it? »Pa-na-ma,« read Little Bear. »This crate comes from Panama, and Panama smells of bananas! Oh, Panama is the land of my dreams!«

He ran home and told Little Tiger. He went on talking about Panama far into the night.

»Everything is much nicer in Panama, you know,« he said. »Panama smells of bananas all over. Panama is the land of our dreams, Tiger. We must start for Panama first thing tomorrow, mustn't we, Tiger?«

»First thing tomorrow,« agreed Little Tiger. »Because we don't have to be afraid of anything, do we, Bear? But we must take my stripy tiger duck with us.« Next morning they got up much earlier than usual.

»If you don't know your way,« said Little Bear, »the first thing you need is a signpost.« And he made a signpost out of the crate.

»We must take my fishing rod too,
because if you have a rod you can always
catch fish, and if you can catch fish you
needn't go hungry...«
»And if you needn't go hungry,« said
Little Tiger, »there's nothing to be afraid
of, is there, Bear?«
Little Tiger took the red cooking pot too.

»So that you can cook me a nice dinner
every day, Bear! Everything you cook
tastes so good. Yum, yum…«
Little Bear took his black hat as well, and
then they set off, going the way the signpost pointed. They walked along the river
bank.

Just a minute, Little Bear and Little
Tiger! Don't you see that letter in a
bottle floating down the river? It might
be a secret message about pirates' treasure! Too late. It's floated past now.
Soon they met a mouse digging a hole.
»Hullo, Mouse,« said Little Bear. »We're
going to Panama. Panama is the land of
our dreams. Everything is different there.
Much bigger…«
»Bigger than my mousehole?« asked the
mouse. »Impossible!«
Well, how can you expect mice to know
anything about Panama?

They passed an old fox, who was just having a goose for his birthday treat. »Which is the way to Panama?« asked Little Bear.

»Turn left,« said the fox, without giving the matter much thought, because he didn't want to be disturbed. Left was the wrong way; they shouldn't really have asked the fox.

Then they met a cow.

»Which is the way to Panama?« asked Little Bear.

»Turn left,« said the cow. »If you turn right you get to the farmhouse, and I'm sure the farmhouse can't be in Panama.«

Left was the wrong way again. If you keep on turning left, where do you get to in the end? Yes, quite correct!

It soon started to rain. Big raindrops kept falling from the sky.

»I'm not afraid of anything so long as my stripy tiger duck doesn't get wet,« said Little Tiger.

Where is your beautiful umbrella, Little
Bear and Little Tiger? You left it at home,
hanging on the door.
That evening Little Bear built them a
shelter from the rain, out of two old oil
drums. They lit a fire and got warm.

»How nice it is to have a friend who can build a shelter from the rain,« said Little Tiger. »With a friend like that, you don't have to be afraid of anything.«

When it had stopped raining they went
on.
Soon they felt hungry, and Little Bear
said, »I've got my rod, so I'll go fishing.
You wait under this big tree, Tiger, and
light a little fire so we can cook our fish.«
But there wasn't any river, and if there
isn't any river a fishing rod is no use.

Luckily Little Tiger was good at finding
mushrooms, or they might have gone
hungry after all.

»If you have a friend who can find mushrooms,« said Little Bear, »you don't have
to be afraid of anything, do you, Tiger?«
Soon they met two people carrying their
harvest home, a hare and a hedgehog.

»Come home with us, do!« said the kind
hare and hedgehog. »You can stay the
night. We like having visitors who can
tell a good story.«

Little Bear and Little Tiger sat on a lovely comfortable sofa.

»This sofa is the most beautiful thing in the world!« said Little Tiger. »We'll buy ourselves a sofa like this when we get to Panama, Bear, and then we shall have everything we could wish for, shan't we?«
»Yes,« said Little Bear.
Then Little Bear told the hare and the hedgehog about Panama. He talked about Panama all evening.
»Panama is the land of our dreams,« he said. »Panama smells of bananas all over, doesn't it, Tiger?«
»We've never been beyond the far end of our field,« said the hare. »Our field has always been the land of our dreams, because it grows the corn we eat. But now the land of our dreams is Panama! Oh, Panama is so wonderful!«
Little Bear and Little Tiger slept on the beautiful sofa, and they all four dreamed of Panama that night.

Next day they met a crow.

»Birds are clever,« said Little Bear, so he asked her the way.

»What way?« asked the crow. »There are hundreds and thousands of ways you could go!«

»The way to the land of our dreams,« said Little Bear. »Everything is different there. Much bigger and more beautiful ...«

»Oh, I can show you the land of your dreams!« said the crow (for birds really are clever). »Just fly after me. Up we go!«

And she flew up to the lowest branch of the big tree. She flew higher and higher. Little Bear and Little Tiger couldn't fly, so they had to climb.

»Don't let go of me, Bear!« cried Little Tiger. »My tiger duck might break a wheel.«

»There you are,« said the crow. »That's it.« And she pointed to the country all around them with her wing.

»Oh, how beautiful!« cried Little Tiger.
»Isn't it beautiful, Bear?«

»It's the most beautiful thing I've ever
seen,« said Little Bear.

But all they were really seeing was the countryside and the river where they used to live before. You can see their little house, over there among the trees. Only this was the first time they had ever seen it from so high up.

»It's Panama!« said Little Tiger. »Come on, we must hurry up! We must reach that river, and build ourselves a nice little house with a chimney. There's nothing to be afraid of, Bear!«

And they climbed down the tree. Soon they came to the river. But where is your boat, Little Bear and Little Tiger? You left it by your little house, down by the riverside.

»You look for some bits of wood and planks,« said Little Bear, and he built a raft.

»How nice it is to have a friend who can build rafts!« said Little Tiger. »With a friend like that, you don't have to be afraid of anything.«

They dragged their raft into the river and
floated over to the other bank on it.

»Go carefully, Bear,« said Little Tiger. »I don't want my tiger duck to capsize. She isn't a very strong swimmer.«

When they reached the other side of the river they walked along the bank. »Just follow me,« said Little Bear. »I know the way!«

»Then there's nothing to be afraid of,« said Little Tiger, and they went on until they came to a little bridge.

Little Bear had once built that bridge
himself; by now they were quite near the
bushes where their own house stood.
But they did not recognize the bridge,
because as time went by the river had
damaged it.

»We must mend this bridge,« said Little
Tiger. »You push the plank from under-
neath, and I'll pull it from on top. But
mind my tiger duck doesn't roll into the
water, because she isn't a very strong
swimmer.«

Look, Little Bear and Little Tiger! There
goes another bottle floating down the
river. There might be a secret message
inside it.

Wouldn't you be interested in real pirates'
treasure in the Mediterranean Sea?
Too late. The bottle has floated past.

On the other side of the river they found
a signpost. It had fallen over and was
lying in the grass.
»What do you see there, Tiger?«
»Where?«
»Here, of course!«
»A signpost.«
»And what do you see written on it?«
»Nothing. I can't read.«
»Pa…«
»Paraguay.«

»No, stupid! Pa-na-ma. Panama. Tiger, we're in Panama. The land of our dreams! Oh, come along, let's dance for joy!«

And they danced for joy, in and out and round about.
But of course, you know what that sign-post was, don't you? Exactly!
When they had gone a little farther, they came to a tumbledown little house with a chimney.

»Oh, Tiger!« cried Little Bear. »You have
good sharp eyes... tell me what you see!«

»A house, Bear. A lovely, wonderful, beautiful house. With a chimney. The most beautiful house in the world, Bear. We could stay and live here, couldn't we?«

»And it's so nice and quiet, Tiger,« said Little Bear. »Just listen!«

Their old house was rather weather-beaten, what with the wind and the rain, so they did not recognize it.

The trees and bushes had grown taller, so everything was a little bigger.

»Everything is much bigger here, Bear,« cried Little Tiger. »Don't you think Panama is a beautiful place?«

They started mending their house. Little Bear built a roof and a table and two chairs and two beds.

»The first thing I need is a rocking chair,« said Little Tiger, »or I won't be able to sit and rock myself.«

And he made a rocking chair.

Then they planted things in the garden,
and soon everything was just as good as
it used to be. Little Bear went fishing,
and Little Tiger went looking for mushrooms. In fact, it was even *better* than it
used to be, because they bought them-
selves a soft, plushy sofa. Then they
thought their little house among the
bushes was the most beautiful place in
the whole world.

»Oh, Tiger,« Little Bear said every day.
»How glad I am we came to Panama!
Aren't you glad, too?«

»Yes, I am,« said Little Tiger. »Panama is the land of our dreams. And we can stay here for ever and ever.«

You think they might just as well have stayed at home all the time?

You think they needn't have taken a trip to Panama at all?

You're wrong. Because then they would never have met the fox and the crow. They would never have met the hedgehog and the hare. And they would never have found out how comfortable a lovely, soft, plushy sofa can be.